GREAT RIVER REGIONAL LIBRARY

BUFFALO BILLS

CREATIVE EDUCATION · NFL TODAY · JOHN NICHOLS

Published by Creative Education
123 South Broad Street, Mankato, Minnesota 56001
Creative Education is an imprint of The Creative Company

Designed by Rita Marshall

Photos by: Allsport USA, AP/Wide World Photos, Bettmann/CORBIS, SportsChrome

Copyright © 2001 Creative Education.
International copyrights reserved in all countries.
No part of this book may be reproduced in any form without written permission from the publisher.
Printed in the United States of America.

Library of Congress Cataloging-in-Publication Data

Nichols, John, 1966–
Buffalo Bills / by John Nichols.
p. cm. — (NFL today)
Summary: Traces the history of the team from its beginnings through 1999.
ISBN 1-58341-037-6

1. Buffalo Bills (Football team)—History—Juvenile literature. [1. Buffalo Bills (Football team)—History. 2. Football—History.] I. Title. II. Series: NFL today (Mankato, Minn.)

GV956.B83N53   2000
796.332'64'0974797—dc21   99-015741

First edition

9 8 7 6 5 4 3 2 1

L ike so many cities along the Great Lakes, Buffalo, New York, is held captive every winter by heavy snowfalls. For years, the citizens of this northern city have looked to sports, especially football, as one way to survive the long, cold winters. But residents of Buffalo have not always been able to see professional football in their city.

In 1950, the All-America Football Conference (AAFC) merged with the National Football League, and Buffalo lost its beloved pro team, which was named the "Bills" in honor of Western legend Buffalo Bill Cody. As a city that thrived on sports, Buffalo was eager to attract another pro

A Bills star of the '60s, quarterback Jack Kemp.

Fullback Cookie Gilchrist set a new AFL single-season rushing record with 1,096 yards.

football franchise. The NFL, however, was not about to grant Buffalo its wish.

Soon, though, Lamar Hunt, a wealthy Texas businessman who made his fortune selling Hunt's Catsup, petitioned the NFL to let him start a new football team. When the league refused, Hunt contacted seven interested friends. This "Foolish Club," as the group of eight risk-takers came to be known, formed a new football league—the American Football League (AFL).

One of Hunt's partners was Ralph C. Wilson, an avid football fan. When Hunt suggested reviving football in Buffalo, Wilson contacted city leaders and signed a lease on the city's War Memorial Stadium in November 1959. Today, more than 40 years later, Wilson and his family still manage the franchise, one of the most consistently successful in the NFL.

A Team at Last

Buffalo's new team did not have a winning season in 1960 or 1961, but it was not because of a lack of fan support. Named the Bills after Buffalo's earlier team, the club got an unexpected "welcome home" parade on July 29, 1960. The day before the Bills' first exhibition game, more than 100,000 cheering fans crowded the streets of Buffalo to welcome their new team.

The Bills' rebirth as an AFL team was directed first by Garrard "Buster" Ramsey, a former guard and defensive coach for the Detroit Lions, and later by Lou Saban, the former Boston Patriots coach. The hot-tempered Ramsey lasted only two years as Buffalo's head man. Lou Saban, who coached

Dangerous wide receiver Andre Reed.

Buffalo scored 20 unanswered points to defeat San Diego 20–7 for the AFL championship.

Buffalo from 1962 to 1965 and again from 1972 to 1976, proved more popular. Saban had been a quarterback at Indiana University in the early 1940s. After serving in World War II, he became a linebacker with the AAFC's Cleveland Browns. After retiring as a player, Saban began a college coaching career in 1950. Twelve years later, he brought his much-needed experience to the young Bills.

As the Bills' head coach, Saban had an amazing ability to find players with hidden potential and turn them into winners on the field. Among those early stars were wide receiver Elbert Dubenion, fullback Cookie Gilchrist, kicker Pete Gogolak, and quarterbacks Jack Kemp and Daryle Lamonica.

Elbert Dubenion, from small Bluffton College, became the Bills' first star. His ability to read defenses, snatch passes out of the air under pressure, and run for additional yardage earned him the nickname "Golden Wheels." It also enabled him to set several Bills pass receiving records.

Fullback Cookie Gilchrist came to Buffalo in 1962 from the Canadian Football League and immediately began dominating the league. The first AFL back to gain more than 1,000 yards in a season, Gilchrist, at 6-foot-3 and 251 pounds, was nearly impossible to bring down as he bulled toward the goal posts. In one stunning performance against the New York Jets, Gilchrist ran for five touchdowns and 243 yards, leading Buffalo to a 45–14 rout.

Pete Gogolak, signed in 1964 from Cornell University, brought a new style of kicking to the AFL. Gogolak kicked the football using a soccer-style kick. Although fans at first found it amusing, his strange method was effective—Gogolak kicked 47 field goals in his two years with the team.

The quarterback duo of Jack Kemp and Daryle Lamonica led the Bills to five consecutive winning seasons between 1962 and 1966. Instead of displaying the usual rivalry between quarterbacks jockeying for the top position, Kemp, the starter, and Lamonica, the reliever, worked together to lead one of the league's most dangerous offensive teams.

Kemp, a 1957 graduate of Occidental College, came to Buffalo in mid-1962 from the San Diego Chargers. Although he appeared in only four games that year with his new team, he ended up in the AFL All-Star game and helped produce a winning season for a team that had begun the year with five straight losses.

In 1965, Coach Saban left to coach at the University of Maryland, and Daryle Lamonica and Cookie Gilchrist were both traded, weakening the championship team. It was the end of an era, but what an era it had been. The seven-year-old Bills had already claimed five winning seasons and two AFL championships.

Quarterback Jack Kemp passed for 2,503 yards and 14 touchdowns.

O.J. AND "THE ELECTRIC COMPANY"

Dismal seasons in 1967 and 1968 dropped the Bills to the bottom of the AFL standings. The only thing fans had to look forward to was the team's number one pick in the 1969 draft. Little did Buffalo fans know that their draftee, Heisman Trophy winner O.J. Simpson, would become one of football's greatest stars.

Orenthal James Simpson, known during his playing days as "O.J." or "the Juice," was the object of every pro coach's attention when he finished college at the University of

Longtime Bills quarterback Jim Kelly.

Dominant defensive end Bruce Smith.

1970

Marlin Briscoe became the first Bills receiver to gain 1,000 yards in a season.

Southern California in 1969. As a senior, Simpson had broken NCAA records for both carries and rushing yards. When balloting was completed for the Heisman Trophy in 1968, Simpson won by the largest point margin ever.

In addition to playing football at USC, Simpson had also been part of the school's world record-setting 440-yard relay team. Because of his phenomenal speed on the track, he was often called "the fastest man in cleats."

While Simpson was a welcome sight in Buffalo, he called his early years in a Bills uniform the "three lost years." Bills coach John Rauch did not share Simpson's love for running the ball. "That's not my style," Rauch said. "I couldn't build my offense around one back, no matter how good he is."

Meanwhile, Simpson felt his skills were getting rusty. He ran for fewer than 700 hundred yards in 1969 and 1970, rarely scored, and watched his team endure three more demoralizing seasons. Simpson pondered quitting the team until Rauch quarreled with team owner Ralph Wilson and soon thereafter left Buffalo. The Bills endured one more losing season before Lou Saban, known as Buffalo's miracle worker, returned to coach the Bills in 1972.

Saban's arrival encouraged Simpson and his teammates. They knew that Saban was tough and demanding, but they also knew that the coach favored the running game and was honest about what he expected from his players. As he told the team after handing Simpson the ball, "There's your meal ticket. Block for him." Behind his teammates' blocking, Simpson ran for 1,251 yards and won the league rushing title in 1972. Even though the team finished with only a 4–9–1 record, morale was definitely on the upswing.

Much of the change in attitude could be traced to Coach Saban's creation of "the Electric Company," an offensive unit designed to turn on "the Juice." Through trades, waivers, and the college draft, Saban gathered an impressive roster of talent. Through the draft, he acquired such players as guards Joe DeLamielleure and Reggie McKenzie and quarterback Joe Ferguson, while other maneuvers brought tackle Dave Foley, center Mike Montler, and receiver J.D. Hill to Buffalo.

The Electric Company demonstrated its power in the December 16, 1973, matchup at home against the New York Jets. Before that game, the offensive line had already led Buffalo to its first winning season in six years. In 13 games, it had also allowed Simpson to rush for 1,803 yards—only 60 yards short of Jim Brown's longstanding single-season rushing record.

Wideout J.D. Hill earned a trip to the Pro Bowl with 754 receiving yards.

Record-breaking halfback O.J. Simpson.

Bob Chandler set a new Bills record with 10 touchdown receptions in a single season.

The game against the Jets was the last game of the regular season. In bitterly cold conditions, Simpson's blockers punched holes in the Jets' defense. By the fourth quarter, O.J. Simpson had broken Brown's record. He had gained 2,003 yards in one season, a record that would stand until 1984. Soon after, Simpson's proud teammates carried him off the field to the roar of the crowd.

The Juice and his offensive line led the Bills to two more winning seasons in 1974 and 1975, and Simpson's impressive list of records grew even longer. But Simpson was unhappy. The Bills' 1976 season ended with a frustrating 2–12 record. Lou Saban's resignation and the departure of such players as receivers Ahmad Rashad and J.D. Hill weakened the Bills.

The last straw fell during an October 30, 1977, game against Seattle that left Simpson with a reinjured knee. He asked to be traded. He wanted to go home, and he wanted the chance to play in a Super Bowl. He got his wish in March 1978 when the Bills' new coach, former Los Angeles Rams skipper Chuck Knox, traded Simpson to the San Francisco 49ers for five future draft choices.

REBUILDING THE BILLS

Although it took him two years to rebuild his new team in Buffalo, Chuck Knox used his time—and the five draft picks he'd acquired—wisely to create a strong defense. Knox already had a strong offense led by quarterback Joe Ferguson, who had blossomed into one of the league's top signal-callers.

Two-time AFC Defensive Player of the Year, Cornelius Bennett.

Joe Ferguson was an intelligent on-field leader.

While at the University of Arkansas, Ferguson had perfected the long-bomb passes that made him the Bills' leading passer from 1973 to 1984. Voted an All-American during his junior year in college, Ferguson was drafted by the Bills in 1973, arriving just as O.J. Simpson's greatest season began. The two became friends, and the great runner taught the young quarterback a few tricks of the trade.

Rugged nose tackle Fred Smerlas was named to a fourth straight Pro Bowl.

The other mainstay of the Buffalo offense was a young running back who joined the Bills through the O.J. Simpson trade. A second-round draft pick, Auburn's Joe Cribbs was a good investment. "I like to call him Joe 'Houdini' Cribbs, as in escape artist," said Bills defensive back Mario Clark. "Even when you get him in your hands, you can't tackle him. He just sort of squirts through your fingers." Cribbs led Buffalo in rushing for four straight seasons and today is ranked third in total yards rushed in a Buffalo uniform.

While the offense carried much of the load, Knox carefully built up his defense. With high draft picks, Coach Knox selected nose tackle Fred Smerlas and linebacker Jim Haslett. Isiah Robertson and Phil Villapiano, two more linebackers, were obtained in trades with the Los Angeles Rams and the Oakland Raiders.

Knox led the Bills to playoff appearances in 1980 and 1981. Although they didn't make it to the Super Bowl either season, the Bills' 31–27 victory over the New York Jets in the 1981 playoffs convinced skeptics that Buffalo was a rising power. The glory years seemed to be returning.

A two-month players' strike and resulting shortened season in 1982 upset Coach Knox's carefully laid plans for rebuilding. The loss of such Bills stars as Joe Cribbs over salary

The Bills rose to greatness in the '90s (pages 18-19).

1 9 8 6

Quarterback Jim Kelly passed for 3,593 yards in his first season as the Bills' starter.

disputes further slowed the momentum that had been building. Discouraged, Knox left Buffalo for a new coaching job in Seattle.

Knox's trusted assistant Kay Stephenson took over as Buffalo's head coach in 1983. Although Stephenson managed to lead his injury-riddled team to an 8–8 record in his first season, neither he nor his successor, Hank Bullough, were able to revive the ailing Bills. The club finished 2–14 in 1984 and 1985 and 4–12 in 1986.

The key in Buffalo's turnaround would be Marv Levy, who was named Bills head coach in 1986. The polite and articulate Levy was a Harvard graduate and brought extensive experience to his new post. Levy, who had spent time as a coach in Philadelphia, Los Angeles, Washington, and Kansas City, was able to quickly redirect the Bills' course. In 1987, he led them to a 7–8 record, and in 1988 and 1989, he took them all the way to the top of the AFC's Eastern Division.

STARS OF THE '90S

Coach Levy was responsible for developing an impressive roster of young players. Defensive end Bruce Smith, a former All-American at Virginia Tech, was among the league's most feared pass rushers. He and linebacker Cornelius Bennett soon became perennial Pro-Bowlers. Free safety Mark Kelso, a free agent who signed with Buffalo in 1986, was one of the top ball hawks in the AFC.

Leading the Buffalo offense was star quarterback Jim Kelly, who had been called "our future" by former coach Hank Bullough. Kelly came to the Bills in 1986 after two seasons with the United States Football League's Houston Gamblers. One of five brothers who played collegiate football, Kelly would be the first in a long line of great quarterbacks from the University of Miami. A popular figure in Buffalo, Kelly had his own radio and television shows.

On the football field, Kelly was one of the game's greatest quarterbacks. Led by Kelly's strong arm, the Bills were the NFL's second-highest scoring team in 1989, topped only by the Super Bowl-bound San Francisco 49ers. The following year, Kelly finished with one of the highest quarterback ratings (101.3) in NFL history and was selected to the Pro Bowl.

Kelly was not the only star—two young players had emerged alongside him to share the spotlight, thus forming the nucleus of the greatest offensive unit in Bills history.

Head coach Marv Levy led the Bills to their first playoff appearance in seven years.

Elusive running back Joe Cribbs.

22 *Thurman Thomas excelled as both a rusher and a pass catcher.*

The first was wide receiver Andre Reed, an unheralded fourth-round draft pick taken by the Bills in 1985. Reed played his college ball at Kutztown University in Pennsylvania—hardly a hotbed for emerging pro football talent. But he quickly established himself as Kelly's favorite long-range target and as a perennial lock for the Pro Bowl. Reed would go on to break virtually every Bills receiving record and rank among the top all-time pass catchers in NFL history.

The second star was running back Thurman Thomas, a second-round draft choice from Oklahoma State in 1988. At 5-foot-10 and 198 pounds, Thomas was relatively small by NFL standards. But that didn't stop him from becoming one of the most versatile—and feared—backfield talents of his era. Equally dangerous as a runner and a receiver, Thomas set a new NFL record by leading the league in total yardage for four consecutive seasons (1989–1992). Like Reed and Kelly, Thomas made frequent trips to the Pro Bowl.

Cornelius Bennett played five different positions in the Bills defense during the season.

Four Straight Super Bowls

With a defense led by Smith and Bennett and an offense starring Kelly, Reed, and Thomas, the Bills clearly had remarkable talent. But what Buffalo accomplished in the first four years of the 1990s was more than remarkable—it was unparalleled in NFL history.

The Bills appeared in four straight Super Bowls. Although they lost all four of those games, the losses did not diminish the team effort and dedication that went into creating such a remarkable streak. Buffalo lost in its first Super Bowl appearance by the narrowest of margins—one point to the New

Bruce Smith had one of the best seasons of his career, posting 108 tackles and 14 sacks.

York Giants. That Super Bowl, played on January 27, 1991, has been called "A Game for the Ages."

In the first half, the two powerhouse teams showed just how evenly matched they were. The Giants began the scoring with a field goal, which was matched by a 23-yard field goal by Buffalo kicker Scott Norwood. Then, in the second quarter, the Bills scored a touchdown on a one-yard plunge by running back Don Smith. This was followed by a safety scored when Buffalo's Bruce Smith sacked Giants quarterback Jeff Hostetler in the end zone. The Giants then countered with an 87-yard scoring drive. Still, Buffalo went into the locker room at halftime with a 12–10 lead.

The Giants opened the second half with another long scoring drive to move in front 17–12. But in the fourth quar-

Fearless special teams star Steve Tasker.

ter, Thurman Thomas scampered 31 yards for a touchdown that regained the lead for Buffalo, 19–17. The Giants came back once more, kicking a field goal to go ahead 20–19 and place the pressure squarely on the Bills, who launched their final offensive drive from their own 10-yard line with barely two minutes left in the game. The Bills marched 61 yards before Norwood lined up for a 47-yard field goal attempt with four seconds remaining. This time, however, he missed—the ball sailed just right of the goal post as the game clock ran out. "That is the way that all Super Bowls ought to be played," one sportswriter summed up after the epic battle.

Placekicker Steve Christie booted 31 field goals—the second-highest season total in club history.

Unfortunately, Buffalo did not fare any better in the next three Super Bowls, losing 37–24 to the Washington Redskins and then twice in succession to the Dallas Cowboys by wide margins—52–17 and 30–13. Those scores alone, however, do not tell the whole story. The Bills had to overcome increasingly stiff competition each year just to return to the Super Bowl.

During the 1992 playoffs, for example, Buffalo came back from a 35–3 deficit to beat the Houston Oilers 41–38. They did so despite the fact that Jim Kelly was sidelined with an injury. Reserve quarterback Frank Reich led a heroic effort that included four Bills touchdowns in less than seven minutes in the third quarter. Andre Reed seemed to find cracks in the Oilers defense on almost every play, catching three touchdown passes within a two-minute span and driving the Buffalo faithful into a frenzy. When Buffalo kicker Steve Christie booted the winning 37-yard field goal in sudden-death overtime, it completed the greatest point-margin comeback in NFL history.

Eric Moulds combined sure hands with blazing speed (pages 26-27).

FLUTIE AND THE FUTURE

All-Pro guard Ruben Brown used his explosive power to dominate the line of scrimmage.

After their 1993 Super Bowl loss to the Cowboys, the Bills rededicated themselves to getting to the top. Unfortunately, many of the team's greats from the late '80s and early '90s would not move forward with them. Kelso retired after the 1993 season, and Jim Kelly followed suit after 1996. Following a 6–10 season in 1997, Marv Levy also decided to step down. The 70-year-old coach had decided it was time for a younger man to lead the Bills. "I leave today with a heavy heart," said Levy. "There is no better place in the world to coach than right here, and you bet I'll miss it."

Replacing Levy at the helm was Wade Phillips, the son of former NFL head coach Bum Phillips. With Kelly gone, the

A tremendous pass rusher, linebacker Bryce Paup.

Bills' number one priority was to find a quality quarterback. Buffalo signed Rob Johnson, a talented young quarterback formerly with the Jacksonville Jaguars, and also picked up 36-year-old former Heisman Trophy winner Doug Flutie. "Rob is our present and our future," Phillips said, "but we brought in Doug to make sure we'd have a veteran ready in case Rob got hurt."

Buffalo's depth at the quarterback position would pay off. In 1998, Johnson played well in the Bills' first five games but was then knocked out with a rib injury in a game against the Indianapolis Colts. Flutie came off the bench with guns blazing. He completed 23 of 28 passes for 213 yards and two touchdowns to lead the Bills to a thrilling 31–24 win.

For Flutie, the victory was exceptionally sweet. The 5-foot-10 and 180-pound quarterback had spent most of his pro career playing in the Canadian Football League because NFL scouts doubted his size and ability. After earning Most Outstanding Player honors six times in the CFL, Flutie finally was given a chance in the NFL. "I've always been too short, too small, or too whatever," Flutie said. "But I've always won football games. That's what I hope people remember."

Bills fans will never forget the thrill-a-minute season Flutie gave them in 1998. With Johnson sidelined, Flutie sparked the team to nine wins in its last 12 games. His exciting, scrambling style left fans wide-eyed as he threw for 20 touchdowns. "Doug's been amazing," said teammate Bruce Smith. "He gives us a little bit of magic, and it's exciting even for us players to watch."

The Bills' magic season ended with a hard-fought 24–17 playoff loss to the Miami Dolphins, but even in defeat, the

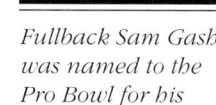

Fullback Sam Gash was named to the Pro Bowl for his great abilities as a run blocker.

30   *Hard-working halfback Antowain Smith.*

Strong-armed passer Rob Johnson.

The Bills counted on fierce linebacker Sam Cowart to lead their defense.

mood in Buffalo remained upbeat. Fans and players alike could sense that positive change was in the air—that the Bills were on their way back to the top of the AFC.

Helping Flutie lead the Bills' charge were two talented young players just beginning to show their potential: powerful running back Antowain Smith and fleet wide receiver Eric Moulds. With this trio leading the way, the Bills soared to an 11–5 record in 1999. The team's defense was the best in the NFL, holding opponents to 10 points or less seven times during the season. Leading the defensive charge were linebacker Sam Cowart and nose tackle Ted Washington, a 6-foot-5 and 350-pound giant known to teammates as "Mount Washington."

In the Wild Card round of the playoffs, Buffalo took on the Tennessee Titans. With just 16 seconds left in the game, Steve Christie booted a field goal to give the Bills a 16–15 lead and an apparent victory. What happened next, however, was simply one of the most incredible finishes in NFL history. Buffalo's kickoff was fielded by a Titans blocker, who handed off to Tennessee's Frank Wycheck. Wycheck then stopped, turned, and fired the ball laterally across the field to receiver Kevin Dyson, who took the pass and sprinted 75 yards down the sidelines and into the end zone. The "Music City Miracle," as the finish was soon dubbed, was a painful end to a fine season for the Bills.

After the season, Buffalo began building for the future by releasing longtime stars Andre Reed, Bruce Smith, and Thurman Thomas. Although Buffalo's roster is changing, its commitment to winning remains the same. The Bills have seen the view from atop the AFC; now they want to stand atop the NFL.